Belly's Deli

R. L. Shafner
Eric Jon Weisberg

Illustrated by Nancy Bauer

Welcome to
The State of
PUNSYLVANIA

Lerner Publications Company • Minneapolis

West Friendship Elem. Media Cent.

To our parents —R.L.S. & E.J.W.
To Mr. Neil, King of the Peanut Butter Meal —N.B.

Copyright © 1993 by Lerner Publications Company

Library of Congress Cataloging-in-Publication Data

Shafner, R.L.
  Belly's deli / R.L. Shafner, Eric Jon Weisberg.
    p.   cm. — (The state of Punsylvania)
  Summary: While investigating the disappearance of food from his deli, Belly encounters many food puns in the speculations of his wife and children.
  ISBN 0-8225-2101-6 (lib. bdg.)
  (1. Delicatessens—Fiction. 2. Food—Fiction. 3. Puns and punning—Fiction.) I. Weisberg, Eric Jon. II. Bauer, Nancy. III. Title. IV. Series: Shafner, R.L. The State of Punsylvania.
PZ7.S52774Be   1993   92-44636
(Fic)—dc20   CIP
                                                    AC

Manufactured in the United States of America

1   2   3   4   5   6   –   P/SP   –   98   97   96   95   94   93

Belly and Nelly worked in the deli. So did their children, Shelly and Jelly. Jelly's real name was Jam.

Belly liked to think that he brought home the bacon by himself, but in fact they all brought home the bacon because they all worked in the deli.

They all lived in the deli, too. They were big livers.

Belly was normally as cool as a cucumber, but lately he felt like he was in a pickle. Food kept disappearing from the deli, and he couldn't figure out what was happening to it.

"I'm becoming a basket case," Belly said.
"Not so long ago we were worth a mint.
Now we're worth peanuts.
Someone in Punsylvania
has sticky fingers."

Jelly and his sister looked at each other. They were afraid. They had seen their father boil with anger, and they didn't want to get into any hot water.

"Dad, I don't want to mince words, okay?" Jelly said. "I think you're full of baloney. Lettuce forget the whole thing."

"Belly," his wife said, "are you sure you've been putting the lox on the door at night?"

"Of course I'm sure," Belly said.
"I don't know," Jelly said.
"That sounds pretty fishy to me."

"Look," Belly said to his family,
"the proof is in the pudding."
He took out a piece of paper
and showed his family the
list of the missing items.

All kinds of salads
were missing—potato,
tomato, macaroni—
and all kinds of meat—
pastrami, salami, and baloney.

"Oh my!" Nelly said, raisin her eyebrows. "What do you think we should do?"

Jelly and Shelly looked at each other again.
Then they looked at the clock.
"Maybe it was Mr. Kelly," Jelly said.
"Mr. Kelly, the band leader?" Nelly said.
"Mr. Kelly is our friend. Besides, that man
is so thin, he can barely lift a drumstick.
How could he take anything?"
"Our son's out to lunch,"
Belly said.

"Mom, Dad," Shelly said, "Jelly's just ribbing us."
"I knew it," Nelly said. She laughed.
"I knew that it wasn't
Mr. Kelly."

"I couldn't help it," Jelly said. "I was on a roll!"

At that moment, the family heard music playing outside. It sounded like Nat King Cole Slaw.

"Hot dog!" Jelly shouted and ran out the door. "Wait!" Shelly called after her brother. "Let me ketchup with you!"

Belly tried to hurry after his children.
But he couldn't cut the mustard,
so he walked with his wife.
"I relish our son's jokes," Nelly said.

Out on the lawn, Belly and Nelly saw long, long tables that went on for miles. And on them was all the missing food. Seated at the tables were all their friends and relatives. They saw the Kellys and the Patellis and the Santanellis. Mr. Kelly was leading the band.

"We've got all the money for the food," Shelly explained. "Everyone wanted to chip in."

Everyone laughed at the surprised looks
on Belly and Nelly's faces.
"Happy anniversary!"
the crowd shouted.
It was Belly and Nelly's
wedding anniversary.

Jelly took out his camera.
"Say cheese, Mom and Dad."

"You're the apple of my eye," Belly said to his family. "You're the core of my existence."
"Now, Dad," Jelly said, "let's not get too corny. There's still more to do."

When everyone had finished eating, Mr. Kelly
again struck up the band. It was a wedding band.

Everyone got up to dance.
Belly led the dance.
It was the belly dance.

Watching her family and friends, Nelly smiled.
She was as pleased as punch.
Then Nelly turned to her son, Jelly.
"Isn't it wonderful," she said,
"to make so many people happy?"

Jelly could tell his mother was getting all
choked up, and he put his arm
around her.

"It's easy to make people happy," Jelly said,
and he winked. "It's as easy as pie."

ABOUT THE AUTHORS

R.L. Shafner has won a number of writing fellowships, including an award from Stanford University. She has published a novella, and one of her stories appeared in *The Signet Classic Book of Contemporary American Short Stories.* She is now writing a novel.

Eric Jon Weisberg's major influences for "The State of Punsyl-vania" are Rocky and Bullwinkle and the Marx Brothers. A graduate of Harvard Law School, he is an attorney for Szold and Brandwen law firm in New York City. He was born and raised in Philadelphia, Punsylvania.

ABOUT THE ARTIST

Nancy Bauer sold her first painting to the Louvre at age 3. At age 10, she received a Ph.D. from the U of XYZ, where she lettered in spelling. When not making appearances on late-night talk shows, she can be found basking in luxury at her seaside villa, La Casa Jumbo (NOT). Nancy is actually a graduate of Minneapolis College of Art and Design, and she currently lives in Minneapolis. She spends most of her time reading, writing, drawing, and tending houseplants.